HEATING UP

Alan Trussell-Cullen

NELSON
CENGAGE Learning·

Australia • Brazil • Japan • Korea • Mexico • Singapore • Spain • United Kingdom • United States

NELSON
CENGAGE Learning™

Heating Up

Fast Forward
Orange Level 15

Text: Alan Trussell-Cullen
Illustrations: Mike Gorman on p.14
Editor: Cameron Macintosh
Design: James Lowe
Series design: James Lowe
Production controller: Emma Hayes
Photo research: Corrina Tauschke
Audio recordings: Juliet Hill, Picture Start
Spoken by: Matthew King and Abbe Holmes

Acknowledgements
The author and publisher would like to acknowledge
permission to reproduce material from the following sources:
Photographs by AAP Image/Rob Elliot, pp 3, 15/ Matthew
Vasilescu, p 22 top; ANT Photo/Grant Dixon, p 9; Getty
Images/Brent Petersen/AFP, p 20/ Peter Essick, p 10/ Jerry
Grayson/Helifilms Australia Pty Ltd, p 6; Istockphoto.
com/Kenneth C Zirkel, p 16; James Ward, p 17 bottom; Lonely
Planet/Ross Barnett, p 6 inset; Newsphotos.com, pp 18-19, 22
bottom/ Nathan Edwards, p 7; Photo Edit/Cindy Charles, p 18/
Anna Zuckerman-Vdovenko, cover, pp 5, 11; Photolibrary.
com/Pearson Doug, p 8/ Robert Houser, p 19/ Dennis
MacDonald, p 13/ David Prince, p 14/ Adrian Weinbrecht, p 17
top/ Photolibrary.com/Age Fotostock/Dennis MacDonald,
back cover, pp 12, 21; Photos.com, pp 4, 23.

ISBN 978 0 17 012606 9
ISBN 978 0 17 012597 0 (set)

Cengage Learning Australia
Level 7, 80 Dorcas Street
South Melbourne, Victoria Australia 3205
Phone: 1300 790 853

Cengage Learning New Zealand
Unit 4B Rosedale Office Park
331 Rosedale Road, Albany, North Shore NZ 0632
Phone: 0508 635 766

For learning solutions, visit cengage.com.au

Printed in Australia by Ligare Pty Ltd
7 8 9 10 11 12 13 20 19 18 17 16

THE UNIVERSITY OF
MELBOURNE

Evaluated in independent research by staff from the
Department of Language, Literacy and Arts Education
at the University of Melbourne.

HEATING UP

Alan Trussell-Cullen

Contents

Chapter 1

GETTING WARMER

Over the last 100 years,
the Earth's temperature went up about
one degree **Fahrenheit**.
In the next 100 years,
it may go up by as much as six degrees.

This rise in temperature is called **global warming**.

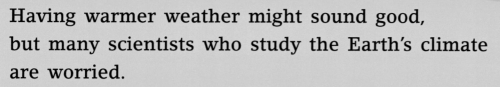

Having warmer weather might sound good,
but many scientists who study the Earth's climate
are worried.
They know that these temperature rises
can make big changes to the Earth's environment.

Chapter 2

GLOBAL WARMING

Global warming can do all kinds of things to the environment.

It can make the weather more extreme.

This means that there could be a lot of hot, dry weather, followed by heavy rain and extreme storms.

Extreme weather like this
could make it hard for people to grow food.

It could also kill a lot of plants and animals.

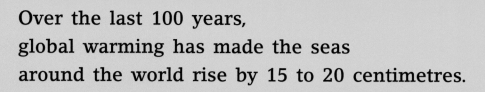

Over the last 100 years,
global warming has made the seas
around the world rise by 15 to 20 centimetres.

Scientists say the seas could rise by
another 100 centimetres in the next ten years.

*People who live near the sea will have
big problems if the seas keep rising.*

This will change the environment
for those who live near the sea.
It will also change the habitats
of fish and animals that live in or near the sea.

Chapter 3

GREENHOUSE GASES

Global warming is not new.
The Earth has been naturally warming
and then cooling for millions of years.

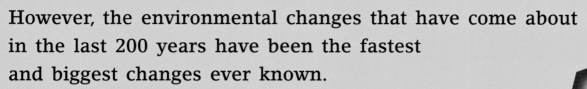

However, the environmental changes that have come about in the last 200 years have been the fastest and biggest changes ever known.

The climate is changing so quickly that most plants and animals will not have time to change along with it.

Many scientists believe these environmental changes come from **greenhouse gases**.

Greenhouse gases are mostly made by humans. They are made when people burn fuel for energy. For example, cars burn fuel that becomes **carbon dioxide**.

Carbon dioxide is a greenhouse gas that most people know about.

There are also many other greenhouse gases that come from the fuels used by power plants and many industries.

Chapter 4

MAKING THINGS HOTTER

A greenhouse is a building made of glass
that traps heat from the Sun.

The glass lets the sunlight in
but keeps the heat from getting out.
This makes the greenhouse heat up.

Greenhouse gases do the same thing to the Earth.
They make a layer of gas around the Earth,
which traps heat from the Sun.
These gases stop the heat from going back into space.
This makes the Earth a hotter place.

Chapter 5

TAKING ACTION

An easy way to cut greenhouse gases is to cut down on the use of energy.

Whenever people turn on a light or watch TV, they are using energy.
A lot of this energy comes from power plants that burn fuel, such as coal or oil.

Whenever people drive cars,
they are using energy that comes from oil.

Everyone has the power to change how much energy they use.

Everyone can:

• buy things that use less energy

• try to use less energy at home

18

• drive cars less – ride a bike, walk or **car pool**.

Many scientists and environmental groups believe that some industries and power plants make too many greenhouse gases.

These groups put pressure on governments to take action about the greenhouse gases made by these industries.

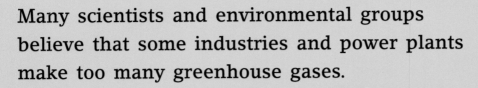

The Greenland Dialogue
-views of climate change

Ilulissat 1   5

Marthinus Christoffel
Johannes van Schalkwyk

World governments met in Greenland, in 2005,
to talk about the problems caused by climate change.

Many governments now have laws that stop industries from making too many greenhouse gases.

People and governments can work together
to help slow down global warming
and the extreme changes it makes
to the Earth's environment.

If the change in climate can be slowed,
then animals, plants and people
will have time to change with it.

Glossary

car pool   organise to drive to work or school with other people

carbon dioxide   a gas that exists naturally in the air. Carbon dioxide is also made when many types of fuel are burnt.

Fahrenheit   a scale to measure temperature. Water freezes at 32° Fahrenheit.

global warming   the gradual rise in the Earth's temperature

greenhouse gases   gases that trap heat from the Sun and make the Earth warmer

Index